STORIES OF
HAUNTED
HOUSES

Russell Punter

Illustrated by
Mike Phillips

Reading Consultant: Alison Kelly
Roehampton University

Contents

Chapter 1

Chillmore Castle

Max Moon was on a school field trip to Chillmore Castle. Everyone was looking forward to the guided tour. Everyone except Max, that is.

He was in a group with Nat and Norm Nuckle. The bullies were always picking on him.

As they waited to go in, the brothers marched up to Max.

4

"You're not brave enough for this, Moon face," sneered Nat.
"Why not?" asked Max.
"Didn't you know, dimbo?" said Norm. "The castle is haunted by a terrifying ghost."

"I don't believe you," said Max, trying to sound brave.

"This way!" called the guide, and the castle tour began.

They climbed to the top of the tallest tower...

and peered into the murky moat.

Yuck!

A secret tunnel in the hillside led back into the castle dungeon.

"This is the very spot where people have seen Sir Hal the Horrible," said the guide. "Wh-who?" asked Max.

"A fierce knight who lived here long ago," she replied. "He's supposed to haunt the castle at midnight."

"Whooah!" yelled Max as a ghostly chill shot down his back. Everyone laughed. Then Max saw why. Norm had put ice cubes down his shirt.

Max didn't dry out until that evening. As the others told ghost stories around the campfire, Nat and Norm grabbed Max.

The twins dragged Max back to the castle and down the secret tunnel to the dungeon.

"Let's see how brave you are now," sneered Norm.

"We dare you to spend the night here alone," said Nat.

"Okay," said Max. The bullies scared him more than a ghost.

"You'll never last the night," said the brothers as they left.

Max soon discovered that the gloomy dungeon was even creepier at night. "There's no such things as ghosts," he told himself.

Just then, Max heard a clanking sound echoing behind him. He turned... to see a ghostly, floating figure.

"Woo, um, I am Sir Hal the Horrible," said the ghost, faintly. "Please beware," he added, in a whisper.

Max couldn't help smiling.

"Kindly leave the castle at once," Hal asked softly. "And do not return... if you don't mind."

Max burst out laughing.

"Don't laugh," begged the ghost. "I'm supposed to be scary."

"I'm sorry," said Max. "You're too friendly to be frightening."

"That's what my boss, King Hugo says," moaned Hal. "I'm not even a real knight. The king says I'm too feeble."

Max felt sorry for the ghost. "Perhaps I can help," he said.

Max spent the night giving the ghost tips on being scary. He told him to...

bellow and boom...

swoop and sway...

and lurch and loom.

"Whew! Where did you learn these scaring skills?" asked the breathless spirit.

"The Nuckle twins scare me all the time," said Max sadly, telling Hal about the bullies.

Max glanced nervously at his watch. "It's time I went out and faced them," he said.

Quietly, Max crept back to his tent – to find Nat and Norm waiting for him.

"I did it," declared Max.

"Don't believe you," said Norm, with a snort.

"You're too much of a wimp," added Nat, shoving Max.

There was a swirl of smoke
and Hal towered over the boys.
"Who dares to shove loyal
Max?" he roared.

The two bullies went as white
as their T-shirts.
"Call him off!" screamed Nat.
"Take him away!" yelled Norm.

"We'll never bully again,"
they promised, terrified.

Suddenly, the ghost of King
Hugo appeared in front of Hal.

"You are now a true knight,"
he declared, placing his sword
on Hal's shoulder.

And, with a wave to Max,
the proud knight and his king
faded away.

Chapter 2

Highwayman's Halt

Polly Small helped her father
run The Highwayman's Halt.
The creaky wooden inn was
over three hundred years old.

But it looked like the Smalls wouldn't be living there for long. They had so few customers they were losing money.

"What will we do?" groaned Polly's dad, as he served lunch to Mr. Trix, the only guest.

"There's always Flintlock's treasure," suggested Polly.

"What's that?" asked Mr. Trix.

"Percy Flintlock was a highwayman who lived at the inn, long ago..." Polly began.

"One night, he robbed a coach and soldiers chased him here."

"Before he was caught, he hid the money somewhere in the building."

"But his bag of gold coins was never found."

"I'm not surprised," Mr. Small said, with a shiver. "They say Percy's ghost will appear if anyone tries to steal his money."

"Ghosts don't scare me," said Polly. "I'll find the treasure."

Mr. Trix smiled sneakily. "Not if I can find it first," he thought.

Polly spent the day searching the inn from chimney to cellar.

All the time, she had the feeling that someone was watching her every move.

Polly couldn't find a thing, not even in the garden. "Percy certainly hid his treasure well," she said.

The ghwayman's Halt

As Polly looked back at the inn she spotted something.

"The sign!" she cried. She fetched her dad's ladder from the shed. Then she climbed up to the carved wooden board.

23

She forced open the lid of the highwayman's chest. Inside was a leather bag.

Flintlock's treasure!

As Polly climbed down, a ghostly figure appeared.

"Hand back my money!" he boomed.

"P...p...please Mr. Flintlock," said Polly, "We really need it."

Percy listened to Polly's tale. "Hmph!" he said, "I suppose I could spare you a coin or two."

"Not so fast, Flintlock!" said a grizzly voice behind them.

"I'll take that!" snapped Mr. Trix. He grabbed the bag from Polly and ran to his car.

"Come back here, you bounder!" barked Percy.

"No way, spooky," shouted Trix as he sped away.

Percy gave a sharp whistle and Polly heard an eerie clip-clopping sound coming closer... and closer...

Suddenly, a ghostly horse galloped around the corner.

"Meet Jess," said Percy. "She's faster than a pistol shot."

"Grab hold of my cloak!" he added. Polly clung on as Percy leapt into the saddle.

"Tally-ho!" cried the highwayman, and they were off.

Percy chased Trix through the town, leaving a trail of chaos behind.

"He's heading for the port," called Polly.

"I know a shortcut!" cried Percy, steering Jess down a back road.

"I'll be on the first boat out of here," laughed Trix as he reached the dockside.

With a bound, Jess leapt out of a side street to block his way.

"I'll push that meddling spook into the sea," thought Trix, driving straight at Jess.

But as Trix zoomed forward, Percy tugged on the reins. Jess floated over the car as it flew off the dock into the sea.

The police dragged Trix from the water, but the gold was lost forever.

Polly didn't mind. Everyone wanted to stay at the inn – and meet the famous ghosts.

Chapter 3

Grimly Grange

Grimly Grange was a crumbling old house full of spiders and spooks. Tourists who popped in got the fright of their lives.

But recently the Grange hadn't had a single visitor.

"I'm bored," said Sir Sidney Snuff one day. "I haven't scared a living soul in weeks."

"Nor me," sighed Miss Lacey. "This is no life for a dead lady."

"Nothing exciting has happened in ages," moaned Darcy Buckle.

Suddenly, Lord Digby Ruff floated in. "Look in the courtyard!" he shouted.

"Who are they?" asked Sir Sidney.

"Who cares?" replied Darcy eagerly. "As long as they're scared of ghosts."

As the visitors explored, the ghosts spied on them from the Grand Gallery.

"It's the Spook Spotters," gasped Miss Lacey.

"Who?" asked Sir Sidney.

"They have a splendid show on the television box," said Miss Lacey excitedly. "They hunt for ghosts. We shall be famous."

"I'll look *so* handsome on the TV screen," boasted Digby.

"Riches!" said Darcy.

"Stardom!" sighed Sir Sidney.

"I can see it now," he added dreamily, "The Sir Sidney Snuff Show…"

"Come my dears, let us get ready," said Miss Lacey.

The ghosts spent the rest of the day preparing for the TV cameras.

They picked out their fanciest outfits...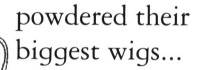

 powdered their biggest wigs...

and polished their best buckles.

Finally they were ready for the show.

With a bong, the clock in the hall chimed midnight. Sue Snoop, the presenter, stood in front of the camera. "Hello viewers," she whispered.

Beside Sue stood Claude Aura, world famous ghost expert.

"Are you sensing any spirits, Claude?" asked Sue.

"Not yet," he replied. "Perhaps this place isn't haunted after all."

At the top of the stairs, Sir Sidney was about to make his entrance. "Not haunted, eh?" he muttered. "Prepare yourself for a shock, sir!"

Sir Sidney jumped on the banister and slid down at top speed.

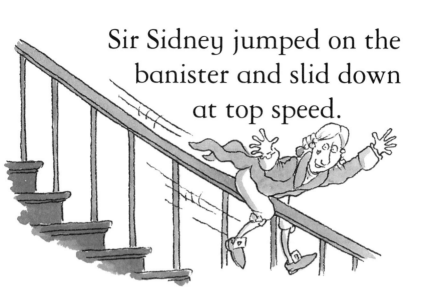

He slid so fast, he flew off the end, across the hall and out of the window.

"Do you feel anything, Claude?" asked Sue.

"Only the breeze from this open window," replied Claude and slammed it shut.

Sir Sidney tried to untangle himself from the bushes.

The disappointed TV crew went into the Great Hall.

Digby and Darcy were already there, hidden in the chimney. "We'll shoot out and scare their pants off," laughed Digby.

His giggling brought down a thick pile of soot. Suddenly, the ghosts were buried up to their wigs.

"What's that?" asked Sue.
"Just a chimney that needs
sweeping," Claude said sadly.
"This is a spook-free zone."

The TV crew moved on to
the ballroom...

...where Miss Lacey was waiting behind a curtain. With a last look in a mirror, she floated out to greet them.

Eek!

But her wig caught on a light. "I'll die of embarrassment if they see me like this," she thought. "And I've already died once."

Miss Lacey ducked back behind the curtain.

"No ghosts here," sighed Claude. "Just a rather silly wig. Let's try elsewhere."

Moments later, the ghosts met in the Hall of Mirrors.

"What a mess we all look," wailed Sir Sidney.

"Oh, the shame," sniffed Miss Lacey, clutching her bald head. "No one must see us like this." Suddenly, the TV crew burst in.

"Ghosts!" yelled Claude.

"Oh yes!" cried Sue.

"Oh no!" screamed the ghosts, and they ran off into the night.

Series editor:
Lesley Sims

This edition first published in 2007 by Usborne Publishing Ltd.,
Usborne House, 83-85 Saffron Hill, London EC1N 8RT, England.
www.usborne.com
Copyright © 2007, 2005 Usborne Publishing Ltd.